POTATO PANTS!

POTATO PANTS
BY TUBÉRTO

LAURIE KELLER

Christy Ottaviano Books

Henry Holt and Company
New York

YES, SHE CREATED
THE BOOK, BUT IT WAS
I—TUBÉRTO—WHO
CREATED THE PANTS!

POTATO IS EXCITED!

(That's why he's doing the Robot.)

I call it
the *PO*-bot
because I'm a
PO-tato.

He's excited because today—

FOR ONE DAY ONLY—

Lance Vance's Fancy Pants Store

is selling . . .

POTATO PANTS!

Potato knows every tater in town will want a pair
so he's there early because, like the sign says,
"ONCE THEY'RE GONE, THEY'RE GONE!"

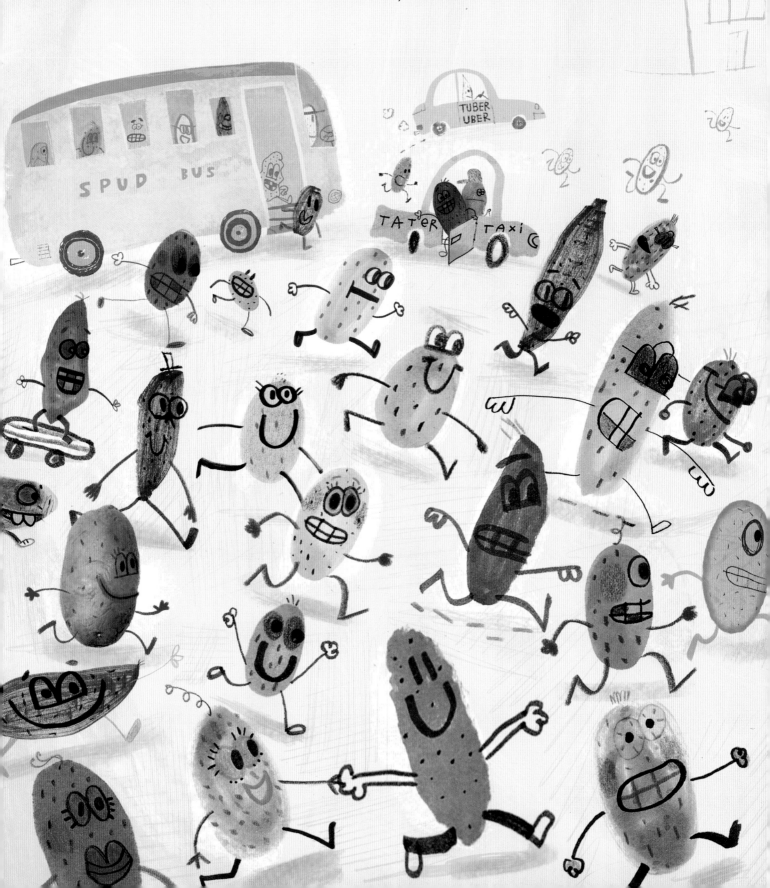

WHAT'S THIS? POTATO IS UPSET!

(That's why he stopped doing the Robot.)

He's upset about that eggplant who just walked into Lance Vance's Fancy Pants Store.

POTATO PANTS!
BY TUBÉRTO

Potato won't go into Lance Vance's Fancy Pants Store now because of that eggplant.

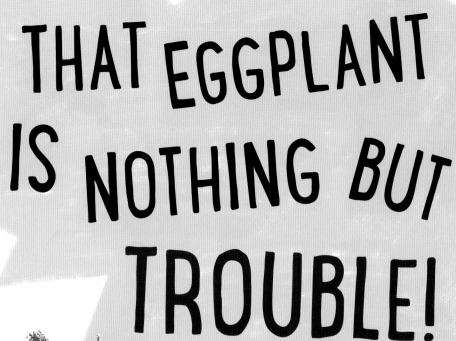

THAT EGGPLANT IS NOTHING BUT TROUBLE!

Yesterday, I was walking along, minding my own potato-y business...

when he ran by and PUSHED ME right into a trash can!

OUT OF MY WAY!!

POW!

If he sees me in Lance Vance's Fancy Pants Store, he'll push me again—

and RUIN MY BRAND-NEW POTATO PANTS!

Poor Potato. It's not easy for him to watch all the other potatoes walk by in their new Potato Pants.

I LOVE my new POTATO PANTS!

We love OURS, too!

Mine have polka dots and ruffles!

Mine have BIG pockets!

Mine are kind of SCRATCHY. I may need some POTATO UNDERPANTS!

Potato is losing his patience waiting for that eggplant to leave Lance Vance's Fancy Pants Store.

What's taking him so long?

And if yesterday was Eggplant Pants Day, why is he here on Potato Pants Day?!

POTATO PANTS DAY— that's RIDICULOUS! Potatoes don't even *WEAR* pants!

It's not "RIDICULOUS," Grocery Store Lady!

OOH! The grocery store!

They have potatoes! Maybe they've got Potato Pants, too!

What a clever potato!

He figured out a way to avoid that
eggplant and still get his Potato Pants!

Potato is not giving up. He's sure there's a way to get Potato Pants without having to face that eggplant!

Only ONE PAIR of Potato Pants left on the rack? What will Potato do now?!

POTATO PANTS!

OUT OF MY WAY!

WHAT A BRAVE POTATO!

He's not going to let that eggplant stop him from getting the last pair of Potato Pants on the rack!

YIKES! Potato may be in for more trouble than he bargained for after that entrance!

Okay, OOOOOKAAAAY,

Potato, let's take a moment here.

Come on, deeeeep breaths...

Inhale...

Exhale...

Inhale...

Exhale...

That's it, think of the puffy clouds...

Inhale...

Exha—

Oh, forget it. This is exhausting! Let it out, Potato...

THAT EGGPLANT RUINED

EVERYTHING!

IT'S HIS FAULT I DIDN'T GET

POTATO PANTS!

HE HAS BRAND-NEW,
PERFECT EGGPLANT PANTS
BUT I'M TOTALLY PANTS-LESS!

IT'S NOT FAIR!

Actually, his Eggplant Pants aren't perfect anymore.

You hit him with the door and they ripped all the way up the back.

You can see for yourself— here he comes.

Oh, Potato! It's been nice knowing you.

Potato is SCARED!

If he had Potato Boots,
he'd be shaking in them.

I'm here to APOLOGIZE.

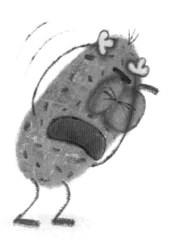

I'm sorry I pushed you. I was in a hurry to get these Eggplant Pants. I hope you'll forgive me.

WHAT?! He's NOT turning me into mashed potatoes?

Potato is **SHOCKED!**

His starchy little head is spinning!

FORGIVE him?

Why should I forgive him—he pushed me into a TRASH CAN!

Errrr…but I ripped his brand-new EGGPLANT PANTS!

Uggghhh, I don't know *WHAT* to do!

So, will Potato forgive that eggplant or not?

I forgive you…
Eggplant.

And I'm sorry for ruining your new Eggplant Pants.

Now **THAT** is **ONE STRIPEY POTATO!**

Potato's favorite thing about
his new Potato Pants—
besides their stripey stripey-ness—
is that they also make GREAT . . .

...ROBOT PANTS!

The End

Meet the Creator of Potato Pants
Tubérto

Tubérto was inspired to create Potato Pants after not being able to find pants that fit him properly. He's now busy designing a full line of potato fashions for both the active and the couch potato.

The Potato Pants Collection

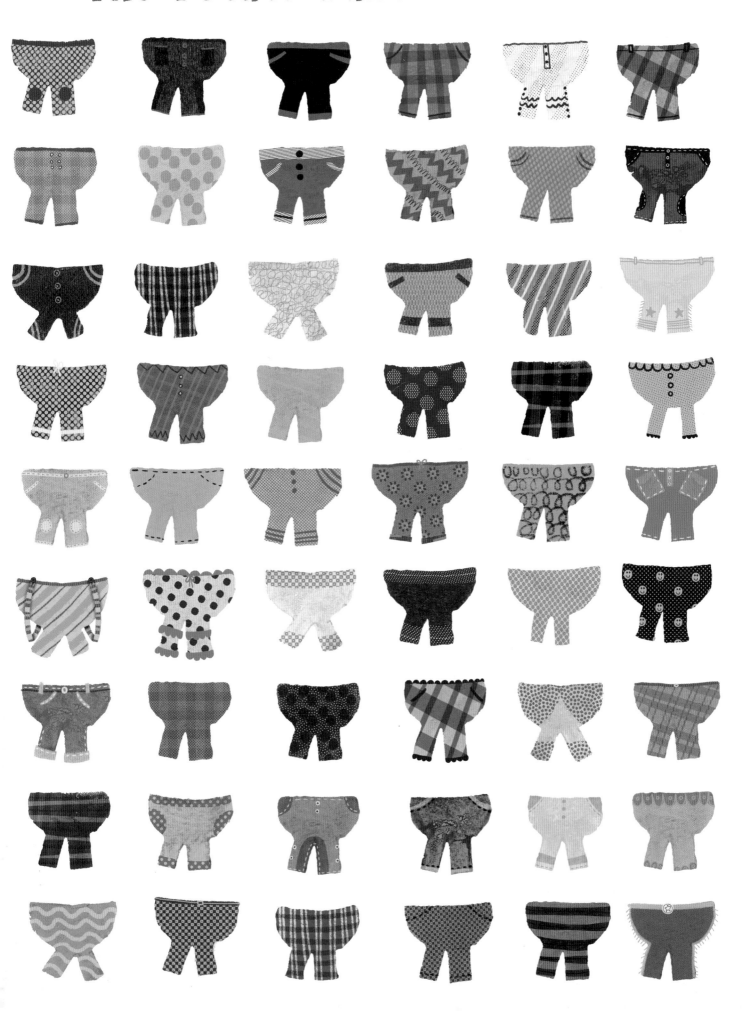

For my Spud-Buds "Critique Group"
Amy, Bob, Charise, and Deb

A thank-you song to my editor, Christy Ottaviano,
to be sung to the chorus of "September,"
by Earth, Wind & Fire:

Otie-O, I hope that you'll remember
Otie-O, January through December
Otie-O, I'm thankful for you every day!

Thank you, Mom and Scott, for your continuous support and encouragement. I yam eternally grater-ful.

And to the uber-tuber talented designer, April Ward—thank you for your keen artistic eye,
never-ending kindness, and extreme patience in dealing with my 247 rounds of revisions!

OUT OF MY WAY, COPYRIGHT WORDS!

Henry Holt and Company, *Publishers since 1866*
Henry Holt® is a registered trademark of Macmillan Publishing Group, LLC
175 Fifth Avenue, New York, NY 10010 · mackids.com

Library of Congress Cataloging-in-Publication Data
Names: Keller. Laurie. author. illustrator.
Title: Potato pants! / Laurie Keller.
Description: First edition. | New York : Henry Holt and Company. 2018. | Summary: Potato is very excited to buy a pair of pants on sale at Lance Vance's
Fancy Pants Store. but when he sees Eggplant. who pushed him the day before. he is afraid to go in.
Identifiers: LCCN 2018004254 | ISBN 9781250107237 (hardcover)
Subjects: | CYAC: Potatoes—Fiction. | Eggplant—Fiction. | Pants—Fiction. | Forgiveness—Fiction. | Humorous stories.
Classification: LCC PZ7.K281346 Pot 2018 | DDC [E]—dc23
LC record available at https://lccn.loc.gov/2018004254

Our books may be purchased in bulk for promotional, educational, or business use.
Please contact your local bookseller or the Macmillan Corporate and Premium Sales Department
at (800) 221-7945 ext. 5442 or by e-mail at MacmillanSpecialMarkets@macmillan.com.

First edition, 2018 / Designed by Laurie Keller and April Ward
The illustrations were created with markers, colored pencils, pen and ink, acrylic paint, potato stamps, collage, and digital drawing.
Printed in China by RR Donnelley Asia Printing Solutions Ltd., Dongguan City, Guangdong Province

1 3 5 7 9 10 8 6 4 2